THE NEXT STEP

THE ROAD TO REGIONALS
BOOK THREE

Adapted By
CHLOE VAN KEEKEN

BEACHWOOD
CANYON
PRODUCTIONS

For information go to **www.beachwoodcanyonproductions.com**

Printed in Canada

First Edition - November 2014

Book Design: Rebecca Lasagna
Cover Design: Yim Hung Kung

ISBN: 978-0-9938500-2-8

CHAPTER 1

Chloe

It had been hard, but Chloe had found a way to manage both work and dance. She had signed up for summer school so that she could take fewer classes during the school year. Then she had convinced her guidance counsellor to arrange her schedule so that she only had classes in the morning. This meant she was stuck dissecting frogs right after breakfast, but it was worth it. With her afternoons free, she could work a shift at the restaurant near her school, freeing her up for dance at four in the afternoon.

After work, she caught the bus across town to *The Next Step* and, during the bus ride, she also got caught up on her homework. Being a dancer meant managing your time very efficiently. Today she was trying to get through a boring novel her English teacher had assigned, when she saw, out of the corner of her eye, Michelle get on the bus. What was Michelle doing on the bus, on her bus?

Chloe sat down in the nearest seat and tried to hide her face with the book. She was still in her waitressing uniform and she didn't want Michelle to see her. If Michelle started asking questions, Chloe wasn't sure what she would say. This was just so embarrassing.

"Chloe?" Michelle asked, sitting down beside her.

Chloe was busted. How was she going to explain this to Michelle? She prayed Michelle wouldn't notice what she was wearing.

"Chloe?" Michelle asked again.

Chloe had to say something. "Oh hey, Michelle! I

didn't see you there." she said, hoping Michelle wouldn't doubt her.

"Okay?" Michelle said, obviously not believing Chloe. "What's with the dress?" Michelle asked.

Chloe looked down at her work uniform and let out a deep sigh. This was her nightmare. There wasn't any way to cover this up. "I have a job." Chloe explained. She may as well tell Michelle the truth and hope for the best.

"Why would you have a job? I have a hard enough time trying to keep up with school and dance." Michelle questioned.

It was now or never. "Well..." Chloe began, "my dad lost his job a few months ago and since A-Troupe is so expensive, the only way I can afford to be part of it is if I help pay for it myself." Chloe looked at Michelle, wondering what she might say. But Michelle only smiled

"That's cool." Michelle said.

"Really?" Chloe was surprised by her response.

"Of course. People our age have jobs. I'm more worried about if you're trying to do too much at once." Michelle said, honestly sounding worried.

"Would you mind not telling anyone?" Chloe asked, hoping she could extend Michelle's kindness a little further.

"I wouldn't. But can I ask why?"

It was a fair question for Michelle to ask. Chloe thought for a few seconds before carefully answering. "Nobody in A-Troupe would really understand what I am going through, and you know how it is with Emily." Chloe explained. "It's either dance or nothing." Chloe hoped this answer would be good enough for Michelle.

"Okay, but you have to give me half of your tips." Michelle demanded.

"You have got to be kidding me!" Chloe protested.

How could Michelle ask her something like that! Especially after Chloe had just told Michelle how much she needed this money!

Michelle burst into laughter. "Of course I am kidding! I would never say something like that!" Michelle giggled.

Chloe began laughing along with her. She had to keep reminding herself that Michelle wasn't Emily. Michelle had been a good friend to Chloe ever since she had joined A-Troupe, so there was no reason for her to doubt that she wouldn't keep Chloe's secret.

CHAPTER 2

Emily

"Dancers listen up!" Kate called to the dancers who gathered around her.

Emily found her place beside Kate. If Kate was going to make an announcement, Emily wanted everyone to think it was Emily's announcement, too.

"For those of you who haven't paid yet, please remind your parents that the cheques for your Regionals' costumes are due tomorrow." Kate told the dancers.

Emily couldn't help but look at Chloe. She knew for a fact that Chloe hadn't paid for her Regionals' costume yet, and in Emily's opinion, that was a big no-no. An E-Girl should always pay her bills on time.

"Emily is going to lead rehearsal today." Kate announced and then headed back into her office.

Emily was glad that Kate was back to letting her run dance rehearsal on her own. She was the Dance Captain after all. "Everyone spread out." Emily called out to the dancers. Why wasn't everyone where they should be for the beginning of the dance? It was like no one here took rehearsal as seriously as she did.

"Hey, Emily!"

She knew that voice anywhere. Emily hadn't really talked to Eldon since duets last week. She couldn't wait to see what he had to say for himself.

"Your shoe is untied."

Emily couldn't figure out why he was telling her this in front of everyone. Emily turned back to the other dancers, but Eldon suddenly bent down and began tying up Emily's shoe. She was horrified.

"What are you doing?" Emily gasped, pulling her foot away from Eldon.

"Tying your shoe for you. Isn't it romantic?" Eldon prompted, looking up at her. Eldon was desperate to make up for choosing Chloe for the duet.

Emily was indeed softening to Eldon, but it was something that was private and not to be displayed in front of everyone. "It isn't romantic. It's weird. Get off." But he didn't move and she had no choice, but to allow him to finish tying her shoe. The dancers snickered, especially the E-Girls who assumed that Emily was not going to tolerate this behaviour.

When Eldon was finished fixing Emily's footwear, Emily decided the best course of action was to just move on with rehearsal and leave the incident behind her. So she started the song *Addicted 2 U*, counted the dancers into the routine, and walked around them, making sure they were in unison.

They were getting close to choosing the Regionals' soloist. Every year one dancer got a featured solo in the Regionals' routine and this week they would be picking a soloist. Emily's eyes moved across the other dancers. James was dancing in his usual goofy way. It bothered Emily, but she knew that when it came down to performance time, he was always on his game. The E-Girls were all dancing well, except for Chloe, whose movements all seemed stiff and uncomfortable.

"Chloe, this isn't cheerleading." Emily called, trying to motivate Chloe along. But it didn't seem to help. She was missing steps and completely out of her spacing. Emily waited until the song ended before she spoke. "Chloe, do you even know the timing?" Emily asked.

"Yeah, of course." Chloe replied.

E-Girl Rule #50

An E-Girl must pay her bills on time.

But Emily wasn't sure. "Steph, show Chloe the timing, please." Emily asked. Stephanie came forward and began breaking down the choreography for Chloe, piece by piece. Emily watched as Chloe followed Stephanie. Chloe was slowly catching on. Everyone else knew the choreography, so why wasn't Chloe up to speed? This wasn't B-Troupe. Chloe couldn't mess around. They had Regionals to think about. The team was only as strong as their weakest dancer.

CHAPTER 3

Michelle

Michelle watched Chloe's eyes go from bright and beaming, to sad and hurt, when Emily began yelling at her for missing steps. Chloe had been distracted, but Michelle couldn't blame her. Kate had just announced that the money for the Regionals' costumes was due tomorrow, way sooner than Chloe had anticipated. Chloe had told Michelle that she had to wait until the very end of the week to get paid, before she could even think about paying for her costumes.

After helping Chloe sneak into the studio to change out of her uniform before anyone could see her, Michelle was starting to understand exactly how hard Chloe had been working to stay in A-Troupe. Michelle felt terrible for Chloe. She had never thought about how much dance cost. The classes themselves were expensive, plus the cost of getting to and from the studio and competitions, not to mention the prices of the costumes for those competitions. Chloe had to love dance a lot to want to keep doing it, even when she had to pay for it herself. Michelle really respected her passion.

But right now Michelle was worried about Chloe. She waited until after rehearsal to pull Chloe aside. She had to make sure everything was okay.

"I've just been working a lot so it's been hard to keep up with everything." Chloe confided in Michelle.

"Have you thought about going back to B-Troupe?" Michelle hated to say it. "If A-Troupe is too much for you."

But Chloe shook her head. "No! A-Troupe is where I want to be." she insisted. "I just didn't know it was going to be this expensive."

Michelle understood. It was a lot to have to take on for a teenager. She knew she had to do whatever she could to try and help Chloe. "What if I help you out?" Michelle offered. "If you have to miss a practice, I can teach you what you missed."

"You want to help me?" Chloe was amazed.

"Of course I do!" Michelle insisted. "Why wouldn't I?"

"That would be really awesome. Thank-you for offering." Chloe said, sounding more than grateful.

Michelle was just glad she could do something. No one should have to go through something like that alone.

CHAPTER 4

West

Both West and Daniel had decided to audition for the Regionals' solo, and both of them had decided to stay late to practise. Getting the Regionals' solo would be amazing for West. As a former B-Troupe dancer, he felt like he still had to prove himself to the rest of A-Troupe. He hoped getting the Regionals' solo would help him do that. Daniel was a strong technical dancer, but West had a style and flair all of his own. And part of that style was making sure there was always a little friendly competition to keep things interesting.

West hooked up his music player to the studio's sound system and turned up the volume on *Talk to the Beat*. He had read the best way to intimidate someone was with sounds and visuals. Might as well give it a try. West began dancing. He popped and locked across the floor, throwing a trick or two into his routine. All to show Daniel that he wasn't kidding around. West backflipped across the floor and, after doing a full twist, landed directly in front of Daniel. "What did you think?" West asked.

"That was good!" Daniel said enthusiastically.

"Yeah it was, wasn't it?" West joked. "You're going to have to work really hard to beat me."

But Daniel just rolled his eyes and continued warming up.

"Remember, I have magic feet." West said, winking at Daniel. Daniel was so serious, West just wanted to make this competition fun. "I'm going to head home… Do you want a ride?" West asked.

"No thanks, I am going to stay and practise a bit longer." Daniel told him.

If Daniel needed more time to practise that was fine. West felt confident in himself, so he was going to go home. "Remember," West said to Daniel, "go big or go home." Daniel smiled at him and then turned on his own solo music. It was a classical piece that was probably very, very old.

But as West headed out of the studio, he began to wonder if Daniel's extra practice was going to be the deciding factor for who got the Regionals' solo. And then West laughed. He had tried to psyche Daniel out, but he wound up psyching himself out instead! Life could be funny that way. Thinking about it made West laugh to himself. He laughed to himself so much that he was no longer psyched out from trying to psyche out Daniel.

Chloe

I t was nice of Michelle to offer to stay late to help Chloe with Emily's choreography. Chloe had been struggling on her own for so long, she had forgotten what it felt like to not have all the weight on her shoulders. Michelle was nothing like Emily had insisted she was. Chloe wondered why Emily disliked Michelle so much. From Chloe's experience, she was kind, thoughtful, and not at all a diva. And it wasn't until Chloe had the routine down cold that Michelle asked her the obvious question.

"Why don't you tell Emily about your situation?" Michelle implored.

"Are you kidding me? I can't tell Emily." Chloe replied wide-eyed. Clearly Michelle hadn't been at *The Next Step* long enough.

"Well, what about Kate? I am sure she would understand." Michelle continued.

"Do you know how many people wanted to make A-Troupe? Giselle is basically waiting at the door. I just have to keep doing what I am doing and hopefully it will get easier." she told Michelle.

"Well, then why don't I help cover for you?" Michelle offered.

"I don't know… you are already on Emily's bad side." Chloe said. Michelle didn't need to get herself into any more trouble with Emily, not for Chloe's sake.

"Exactly. So who cares if she gets mad at me, she's already mad at me most of the time anyway." Michelle joked. "Besides, you don't have a choice. I'm covering for you whether you like it or not." Michelle said firmly, not inviting any more discussion.

"Thank-you so much." Chloe said finally. It certainly felt good to have someone have her back.

"It's not a problem at all." Michelle said, bringing Chloe into a hug.

"Seriously, thank-you." Chloe beamed at Michelle. Michelle was nothing like Emily and that was a good thing.

"Do you want to run through it, one more time?" Michelle asked.

"Sure." Chloe said. Michelle turned on the music and they began dancing. And for the first time in a long time, Chloe felt free to just dance.

Riley

Riley had overheard Michelle's offer to help Chloe with Emily's routine, so she had snuck into Studio-A to watch. Riley was shocked to find out that Chloe was having a hard time at dance, but she was so impressed with how Michelle had handled the situation.

Riley texted James to meet her in *Squeezed* so she could tell him what she had seen. James agreed. For him it was just more proof that Michelle should be Dance Captain. And Emily should be de-throned, but they couldn't figure out how to convince Michelle of that. Riley wanted to wait until the right moment to approach her, but when they saw Michelle walk into *Squeezed*, James decided now was as good a time as any. They got up from their table and approached Michelle.

"Hey, guys!" Michelle said brightly.

Riley hoped this would go over better than the last

time they had asked for her help.

"Oh hey, Michelle." James said, pretending to have just seen her. "How long have you been here?"

"I just got here." she told them.

"Right, of course." James said, nudging Riley to begin.

"So, I saw you talking to Chloe this afternoon," Riley began, "and I saw you working with her after practice."

"That was awfully leader-ish of you." James said.

Riley wished he would have a little more tact.

"I was just trying to be kind." Michelle explained.

Didn't Michelle see that was exactly why they wanted her to be Dance Captain? "Kindness is a great skill to have as a Dance Captain." Riley said, hoping she could get through to Michelle.

"I really don't want to be Dance Captain. You guys have to understand that." Michelle said.

Riley understood that Michelle was scared, but why wouldn't she consider it? "Would you just think about it? Seriously think about it." Riley pleaded with Michelle.

"I did seriously think about it." Michelle snapped.

"No you didn't, not seriously." James said, stepping in. "You have to believe in yourself."

"I do believe in myself." Michelle insisted. "But things

have just settled down with Emily."

"Things will never settle down completely with my sister. They will always boil back up again." Riley was desperate for Michelle to see her side of things.

"We know you are the right choice." James said, trying to sway Michelle.

"You'd be perfect for Dance Captain, but you have to replace her now. Before things get worse." Riley begged.

"No!" Michelle shot at them, getting up and heading out of *Squeezed*.

"We're not going to give up!" James called after her.

Riley nodded; they weren't giving up until Michelle agreed to become Dance Captain.

Daniel

D aniel was in the zone. He had rehearsed until late last night, and he had spent all morning preparing for his solo audition. He followed the same routine every time he had a big dance performance, and that morning had been no different.

He woke up early, went for a quick jog around the block, drank a glass of water, ate a bowl of oatmeal, drank another glass of water, and then grabbed a banana for the ride to the studio. His dad always let him play his audition song in the car on repeat, so he could practise his routine in his head. Then, when he got to the studio, he did ten jumping jacks in the hallway before heading into Studio-A.

"Here we go dancers!" Kate announced.

Daniel took a deep breath. Auditions were beginning. And Daniel knew getting the Regionals' solo wasn't only an honour, it was a glorious opportunity. Representatives from all the big dance schools were known to attend the *Absolute Dance Regionals* competition. And they would be scouting for new talent. It was Daniel's dream to dance at *Juilliard*. Getting the Regionals' solo was the first step towards his future, and Daniel couldn't wait to take it. But first, he had to watch West perform.

As West danced to *We Do It Big*, he moved in a way Daniel had never before seen. He danced like he was making up the choreography as he went. His legs seemed to have springs built right into them. West moved his arms around his head in such a fluid motion that Daniel wondered if his shoulders were double jointed. When West jumped, he flew off the floor with almost no effort. Like magic, Daniel thought.

"Good luck trying to beat that." West said, coming off the dance floor, a little out of breath.

"You and your magic feet should watch this." Daniel said as he took the floor. He was ready to show everyone in A-Troupe that he deserved the Regionals' solo.

As Daniel's song, *Turn me Around* began, Daniel moved along to it, showing off his proper ballet technique. Daniel wanted to show Miss Kate how dynamic he could be. He came out of his side tilt and prepared to jeté across the floor. He launched himself off his right leg, doing a side split as he jumped.

But when he landed, he felt his left ankle give out.

He stumbled, but quickly regained his balance hoping no one else saw him hurt himself. If Kate knew he was injured, there was no way she would choose him as the Regionals' soloist. He quickly finished his routine, trying his hardest to hide his pain. This was not good.

CHAPTER 8

Michelle

Michelle was having a great time watching the Regionals' solo auditions, but she was also worried about Chloe. She was only supposed to be fifteen minutes late, but that was half an hour ago. Michelle hoped Chloe would show up before it was her turn to audition for the Regionals' solo.

"Next up on my list is Chloe." Kate announced, looking around to find her.

It was too late. Michelle knew she had to cover for Chloe. "She's at a doctor's appointment." Michelle piped up, hoping that would adequately explain her absence.

"She's late again? That's disgraceful." Emily spat.

Michelle bit her tongue and wished she could tell Emily that her behaviour was disgraceful.

"That is enough, Emily." Kate said, and then turned back to Michelle. "We can't really wait for her." Kate explained.

"Let me call her. I am sure she's almost here." Michelle said, hoping she was right. She ran across the floor to the cubbies and grabbed her phone as Tiffany took the floor to audition. Michelle wished she could watch Tiffany's performance, but she knew getting hold of Chloe was the most important thing.

"Hello?" Chloe answered on the third ring.

"You have to hurry back," Michelle said quickly, "Emily is catching on and Kate just called your name to audition for the Regionals' solo."

"We got slammed today. I'll just stay another fifteen minutes and then I'll get on the bus. I will be there in an hour, I swear."

"Okay, but hurry." Michelle pleaded with Chloe. She wasn't sure she could cover for Chloe for an entire hour.

"I will." Chloe promised before hanging up.

Michelle stayed where she was, trying to think of what to say to Kate. She missed both Tiffany's and James's auditions, but helping Chloe was more important.

"Michelle?" Kate called from across the floor.

Michelle tried to think of something to say before she got back to Kate, but all she could come up with was, "She will be here any second, Miss Kate."

"She's missed the whole audition anyway." Emily sneered.

"I said she'd be here any minute." Michelle spat back.

"She still missed the whole thing." Emily said, staring down Michelle.

"Emily's right, Michelle. I can't wait for Chloe any longer." agreed Kate.

Michelle understood Kate couldn't wait around for Chloe if she was going to be late, but she felt bad. It wasn't Chloe's fault she couldn't be there, and now she was missing out on a huge opportunity.

"I've decided who is going to be awarded the solo feature." Kate told them. "The dancer is going to be…" she paused for dramatic effect, "Daniel!" she finally announced.

Michelle clapped with the other dancers. She was proud of Daniel, he definitely deserved the solo.

"James. Your audition was also very impressive. You will be Daniel's understudy… So maybe you should learn the routine as well." Kate asked.

Everyone applauded, including Michelle, but she couldn't help but feel bad for Chloe.

Chloe

Chloe hated being late, especially to dance. It was hard enough paying for dance, but now she knew she would have to pay for being late, too. Recently, it seemed like Emily's favourite pastime was making Chloe miserable. When Chloe ran into Studio-A nearly an hour late, she thought she was prepared for Emily's anger, but she was wrong.

"Chloe!" Emily called, pointing out Chloe's entrance to everyone in Studio-A.

Great, Chloe thought, so much for trying to sneak in unnoticed. Why did Emily have to make everything such a big deal?

"Thanks for finally joining us." Emily said, but she didn't sound thankful at all. "But the solo auditions are over," Emily continued, "so you shouldn't have even bothered showing up."

"I'm sorry!" Chloe began, "I had some things I had to

take care of." But nothing Chloe said was going to stop Emily.

"I'm not sure you are aware, but this is A-Troupe." Emily pointed out.

"Yeah, and Miss Kate wouldn't have put me here if she didn't think I could do it." Chloe replied, her voice wavering.

"She wouldn't have put you here either, if she knew you were going to be so late most of the time."

Up until now, Chloe had thought Emily was her friend, but now she was acting more like a bully. "I deserve to be here." Chloe said, using the last bit of courage she had left.

"Really?" Emily snarled. "Because I think you deserve to be in B-Troupe."

"That's enough!" Chloe heard Daniel say. He never had any time for drama and right now Chloe appreciated that. "Can't we get back to rehearsal?" he asked.

"I would love to get back to rehearsal. Why doesn't Chloe show us the moves?" Emily said, glaring at Chloe.

"I don't know them." Chloe finally admitted. Chloe felt like Emily had just punched her in the gut.

"I know you don't know them." Emily spat. "You are behind in everything."

"I am here because I love to dance. Dancing is what I have wanted to do since I was little. It will always be my passion." Chloe said. She was crying, but right now she didn't care.

"Maybe it's time for you to find a new passion." Emily suggested, as if it were that easy.

That was the last straw. If Emily wanted Chloe to leave A-Troupe, then Chloe would leave A-Troupe. She grabbed her bag and ran out of Studio-A, tears streaming down her cheeks. Emily always got what she wanted.

CHAPTER 10

Michelle

M ichelle felt sick. It wasn't fair that Chloe didn't have enough money for dance. Everyone should be able to dance, no matter what. But it was Emily's behaviour that was really churning Michelle's stomach. She had stood by for weeks now and watched Emily walk all over A-Troupe. From Riley to Eldon and now Chloe, Emily left destruction in her wake. But this was the last time she was going to get away with it.

"You know you don't have to be so mean!" Michelle said, stepping up to Emily. "She missed the audition, it's not that big of a deal. Daniel will make a great soloist."

"It's not just the auditions, Michelle." Emily said, taking a step towards Michelle. "She comes late, she leaves early, she's not dedicated. This is A-Troupe."

Michelle was getting tired of hearing Emily say that. She may as well call it E-Troupe. "No one deserves to be treated that way. Do you even know all the facts about

Chloe's situation? Do you know what's going on in her life?" Michelle countered. She wasn't giving up the fight, not this time.

"No. I don't know what's going on in her life, do you?" Emily said with a sneer. "Because if you do, why don't you tell everyone?"

Michelle looked Emily dead in the eyes. Michelle realized she had promised not to tell Chloe's secret, and while revealing the truth would likely make everyone understand, it was Chloe's secret to tell.

"Look," Emily said, getting in Michelle's face, "this is an E-Girl thing."

Michelle laughed. Emily couldn't be serious. This girl was something else. The E-Girls didn't exist in a separate universe. "An E-Girl thing?" Michelle retorted. "Really? Because to me and everyone else in this room, it sounds more like a mean girl thing." Michelle folded her arms. She wasn't backing down now.

"So what are you going to do about it?" Stephanie said, stepping in front of Emily, staring Michelle down.

Michelle thought about it for a second. Without being able to reveal Chloe's situation, she didn't know what else to say. She suddenly felt all alone, standing there challenging Emily. There was nothing she could do. At least not right that second.

"I can't do anything. But I don't have to stay here and watch you girls be bullies." Michelle whipped around and stormed out of Studio-A, hoping her ponytail hit one of them on her way out.

Michelle had left the studio. She had also left her dance bag, and her street clothes, and her school bag. But she didn't care. She had her phone, so she could call her mother to come pick her up. Because there was no way she was going to go back into that studio with Emily around. It wasn't that she was afraid to see Emily. Emily making fun of her, or Emily trying to ignore her, or Emily shooting her looks; none of that bothered Michelle.

Michelle didn't want to go back into Studio-A, because she was really angry. She was so angry that if she saw Emily, she wasn't sure what she might say or do. And she didn't want to act out of anger. She wanted to be able to think through what had just happened, and then figure out what was the best thing to do. Michelle had no idea what that was, but she knew she would figure it out. She always did.

CHAPTER 11

Riley

Riley sat with James in *Squeezed* going over yesterday's events. First Emily had yelled at Chloe and made her cry, and then she had pushed Michelle so far that she may have left *The Next Step* for good.

"There's no one else who will be able to challenge Emily." James said.

"Um?" Riley said, reminding him.

"Other than you, of course. But you don't count, you're her sister." James said joking.

"Great, thanks." Riley said, trying to hide her smile. Even though she was stressed out, she appreciated James's attempts to calm her down. "We still don't know if she's gone, not for sure." Riley said, hopefully.

"She just left. She didn't even take her things. And if she doesn't come back, our whole plan is ruined." James said, worried.

"If who doesn't come back?" Riley heard. She looked up and saw Michelle standing beside their table, holding three juices. She set down a juice in front of each of them.

"What's up?" James casually asked. James never lost his cool, even in the worst situations. Riley sort of admired him for that.

"Do you still want me to be Dance Captain? I'm sick of Emily's attitude." Michelle stated calmly. "It is time for someone to step in and be a true leader."

"Are you that true leader?" James asked, hopefully.

"I'm willing to be." Michelle said, looking back and

forth from Riley to James.

Finally Riley smiled. She was so relieved. Change was coming. "So, what's our plan?"

"What if we re-choreograph the Regionals' routine? Make it better than Emily's routine ever could be."

"Yeah," Riley agreed, "and then we could show it to Kate and Chris. After that, they'd have to make you Dance Captain. Especially if everyone's on our side."

"I'm down. When do we start?" James asked.

"No time like the present." Michelle said, committed.

"To the end of Emily." James said, raising his juice glass.

"To the end of Emily." Michelle said, raising her drink to meet James's.

For a moment, Riley wondered how she and her sister had become so divided. It wasn't long ago that Riley was following Emily around wanting to be exactly like her. But Emily had changed since Michelle arrived, or was it just that Riley saw Emily in a different light? Riley decided she just wanted to be herself, and no one else.

"To the end of Emily." Riley said. And the three friends cheered.

CHAPTER 12

Emily

E mily liked being at the studio before everyone else got there. It gave her time to come up with choreography. She knew exactly how she wanted *The Next Step* to look at Regionals. She was in the middle of choreographing when she heard Kate's voice.

"Emily, can you come in here please?" Kate yelled from the office.

Her tone made Emily cringe. What have I done this time? Since Michelle arrived, it seemed like Emily was being called into Miss Kate's office every other minute.

"Can you make this quick, rehearsal is going to start soon." Emily said, hoping to cut the discussion short. She didn't want to be seen getting yelled at by Kate and Chris.

"We know you're upset with Chloe for being late, but you need to take it easy on her." Kate wasn't happy that a dancer was showing up late, but there were better ways to handle it than how Emily apparently had.

"I know Chloe is my friend, Kate, but she should be here on time." Emily said matter-of-factly.

"Have you bothered to ask her why she's been late?" Kate asked.

"I would love to ask her, if she was ever here."

"Well, you know what you can do when she gets here… apologize." Chris said.

"No." Emily said. She did not apologize.

"You are apologizing, end of discussion." Chris said.

"End of discussion, I'm not apologizing." Emily replied

back, just as firmly.

"Emily, if you want to continue as Dance Captain, you will apologize." Kate said, laying down the law.

"You're not serious." Emily countered.

"I mean it." Kate said, sternly.

Emily scoffed. Why should Emily apologize to Chloe? Chloe was the one who should be apologizing to Emily, and to the entire team for that matter. If Chloe hadn't been late so often, none of this would have happened. But Emily knew which battles were worth fighting, and this one wasn't.

"Fine, I'll apologize," Emily said, then added, "but I won't mean it." She knew she probably shouldn't have added that last line, but she didn't like being forced to do something in which she didn't believe.

Emily stormed out of the office and out of Studio-A altogether. How could Kate and Chris not understand what was best for the team?! It was best for the team if everyone showed up on time, ready to rehearse. It was best for the team if everyone respected the Dance Captain. It was not best for the team if her leadership was challenged. They were being very short-sighted.

6:36PM

Messages **Stephanie** Details

6:32PM

Kate said I have to apologize to Chloe.

Maybe you should. She was really upset.

Whose side are you on?

Yours obviously <3 It will just keep Miss Kate happy.

CHAPTER 13

Chloe

Hanging out with Daniel and West, the other former B-Troupe dancers, made Chloe feel a lot better. Since they had all come up through B-Troupe to A-Troupe together, they had a special bond that Chloe didn't feel with the other A-Troupe dancers. But that bond also meant Daniel felt comfortable enough with Chloe to ask about her recent absences.

"I am not taking Emily's side or anything, but I just don't understand why you've been so distracted lately." Daniel probed.

She wanted to tell him the truth, but she couldn't. Just then Giselle entered the juice bar. "Hey, Giselle." Chloe said. "Don't you have a rehearsal to be at?" Chloe asked, trying to change the subject. Giselle turned around to check the clock on the wall of *Squeezed*.

"Yeah, I guess I should go." Giselle said, giving Chloe a funny look before heading out.

"Why are you dodging my questions?" Daniel asked after Giselle had left.

It was typical Daniel, Chloe thought. He never knew when to let things go. Chloe tried to think of an answer, but she didn't have to think long.

"Chloe?"

Chloe didn't have to turn around to know that sickly sweet voice. Last night she even had a nightmare with that voice in it. A talking strawberry, sounding like Emily, had yelled at her for buying the wrong pointe shoes.

"Could I talk to you for a minute?" Emily asked, extending her hand to help Chloe out of her seat.

"Sure?" Chloe said, hesitantly standing up to face Emily. Chloe wasn't sure what was going on. It hadn't even been twenty-four hours since Emily had made Chloe cry.

"I just came to apologize." Emily said.

Chloe was stunned. She had never heard Emily apologize to anyone. Chloe heard Daniel choke on his drink behind her. Hearing Emily say she was sorry was a first for all of them.

"What I did was really unprofessional and mean. I'm sorry. You are part of A-Troupe, you are an amazing dancer, and you are also an E-Girl." Emily said, squeezing Chloe's hands.

Emily must really be sorry. It takes a lot of courage to stand up in front of other people and say that you were wrong.

"E-Girls for life?" Emily said, forming her hand into the e-shape that each E-Girl knew how to make. Chloe did the same, and she and Emily did the secret E-Girls' handshake.

"E-Girls!" Chloe agreed. It was a relief to be back on Emily's good side. Chloe felt like now it might actually last.

CHAPTER 14

Emily

"Does anyone know where Michelle, James, and Riley are?" Chris asked the A-Troupe dancers. Emily looked around. First Chloe, now Michelle, James, and Riley were late to rehearsal? Did anyone take A-Troupe seriously?

"I think I saw them in Studio-B." Eldon said.

Late, and all together, Emily thought. This was very curious. As Chris headed out of Studio-A to find the missing dancers, Emily pulled Eldon aside. Maybe he knew what they were up to in Studio-B. "Hey, Eldon, do you want to get a water with me?" Emily asked him. It was so easy to get information out of him that all she had to do was offer to spend time with him. "So I was wondering if you could tell me something." Emily asked Eldon, as he handed her a cold bottle of water from the cooler.

"Anything." Eldon offered, eagerly.

"What did you see in Studio-B?" Emily queried, acting as innocently as she could.

"I was just walking by and saw James, Riley, and Michelle." Eldon answered.

"Were they sitting or standing?" Emily asked, prying.

E-Girl Rule #27

Don't keep secrets from E-Girls, it never works.

"They were standing."

"In a formation?" Emily said, nearly tripping over her words trying to get them out fast enough.

"I don't know?" Eldon responded, like his answer was a question.

He clearly didn't understand what she was asking. Emily should have known better than to ask Eldon anything. The only things he paid attention to were Emily and dance. Besides, there was no way he would be able to keep a secret from her. And there was no way he ever would.

CHAPTER 15

Michelle

Michelle hadn't had this much fun at dance since her first days at *The Next Step*, before everything with Emily had gotten out of hand. She was having a great time working with James and Riley on the choreography for their new routine. Michelle would suggest an idea and then Riley and James would add on to it, making it ten times better than it was. They had only been dancing for an hour, but they had already come up with half of their routine.

"At the part when Riley and I are doing the floor work, why don't you do some hip-hop stuff?" Michelle suggested to James.

"Yeah, I could do the coffee grinder and then worm up to meet you guys for the salsa section!"

"Yeah!" Michelle and Riley said in unison, before they broke out into giggles. Working with Riley and James was amazing. Michelle was finally starting to feel like she really belonged at *The Next Step*. At least this version of *The*

Next Step. It wasn't until Chris came into Studio-B that they were reminded that this wasn't exactly A-Troupe. Not yet, anyway.

"Riley, James, and Michelle." Chris said. Michelle looked at Riley and then at James. Had Chris seen their new routine? Was their plan over before they had a chance to put it into action?

"Rehearsal is in Studio-A." Chris said after a few moments.

Michelle let out the breath she had been holding.

"Oh, we were supposed to be in Studio-A!" James said, winking at the two girls. "We were wondering where everyone was! For some reason we thought it was here today."

Michelle wasn't sure if Chris believed James, but if he didn't, Chris didn't let on.

"No. So let's get back there, shall we?" Chris suggested.

"Right!" Michelle said, hurrying out the door right behind James and Riley, thankful that they hadn't been caught.

CHAPTER 16

Emily

"Welcome to class. Thanks for joining us." Emily said sarcastically as Michelle, Riley, and James came into Studio-A with Chris. "It actually started five minutes ago, but thank-you for taking the time out of your lives to fit us into your busy schedules." Emily was tired of people disrespecting her, and she was tired of people disrespecting A-Troupe.

"Emily." Chris said, warning Emily. "Why don't we all get into our first positions? I want to see you guys perform full out this time." Chris said to the dancers, taking control away from Emily.

Emily hated it when Chris took over, especially when he did it front of everyone. Didn't he understand how embarrassing it was for her? Emily took a deep breath, she had to focus on the routine. She could deal with Chris later.

As *Addicted 2 U* began, Emily, Riley, and Tiffany moved across the floor. They met Michelle, Chloe, and Stephanie in the middle. The boys joined them from the

back row as Emily walked towards them. Her favourite part of the choreography was the lift she had given herself in the middle of the dance. As the boys lifted her off the floor, she felt like she was back in her rightful place, looking down on everyone.

As her feet touched the floor, she quickly found her spacing and then all of A-Troupe launched into the group section of the routine. Emily could tell they weren't all in time with each other. All of the boys were dancing lazily as if they were bored. Riley, Michelle, and James were behaving particularly oddly. They didn't seem totally present. If the rest of A-Troupe wasn't committed, then why was Emily wasting her time?

E-Girl Rule #30

And E-Girl is 100% committed to everything she does.

CHAPTER 17

James

James had never been so glad to finish A-Troupe rehearsal. He couldn't wait to get back to Studio-B to keep practising the secret routine with Michelle and Riley. Not only did he get to spend more time with Riley, but he also had the satisfaction of knowing that when they were done, Emily would no longer be Dance Captain.

They were halfway through their new routine when West walked into Studio-B. James, Riley, and Michelle all stopped dancing at once. How much had West seen? As well as West and James got along, West was new to A-Troupe, and it would be a disaster if Emily somehow found out about this.

"What are you guys doing in Studio-B?" West asked, looking puzzled.

"What are you doing in Studio-B?" James asked him back, hoping it would confuse West.

"This is where I keep my extra socks." West replied. "Do you guys keep your socks in here, too?"

"No, West, we don't keep our socks in here."

"That's good, because I wouldn't want to accidentally grab socks that weren't mine." West said earnestly.

James rolled his eyes. West was a weird dude. Why wouldn't West just keep extra socks in his cubby in Studio-A? No matter, there was no explaining West.

"Then what are you guys doing in Studio-B?" West asked again.

James looked at Riley and Michelle. They were

all thinking the same thing. Should they invite him into their dance? If they were going to prove to Miss Kate that Michelle should be Dance Captain, they were going to need more people on their side. It was risky though, because they hadn't worked it all out yet.

"We have something to show you." James said, deciding for all of them.

"All right." West said happily. West could be so weird sometimes it was hard to know how he was going to respond to anything.

James hit play on the stereo and *Addicted 2 U* started playing. It was the same song Emily was using for her routine. They had chosen it on purpose, because they wanted to show everyone that there were other ways to choreograph a dance. They wanted to prove to West that their dance was better than Emily's. When they were finished, they broke out of their last pose.

"That's all we have so far." James explained.

"What do you think?" Michelle asked.

James, Riley, and Michelle all stared at West. This was the moment of truth. If West decided to join them, they were on their way to getting the other dancers on their side. But if West decided not to join them, they'd know that their plan would never work.

"What's the dance for?" West asked.

"It's the new Regionals' routine." Michelle answered.

"Do you know what we're saying, West?" Riley added.

West thought for a moment and then spoke. "Let me get this straight," West began, "you guys are choreographing this routine to show to Kate, to overthrow Emily, so that Michelle can become Dance Captain. Is that right?"

James had to admit that when West said it like that, it

did sound a little far-fetched.

"That's right." Michelle said, sounding like their leader.

West stared at them all. They could not tell what he was thinking. Their entire plan could be over, before it even began.

Then he broke the silence. "I LOVE it!" West sang.

What a relief. Of course West would love their routine. Why wouldn't he?

"I even have some ideas. How about a little hip-hop in the group part?" West asked. He began moving his arms around in an intricate motion.

"Okay, but you're going to have to teach us because I can't do that." Michelle said, laughing.

"Me either." Riley said.

West began showing them some basic tutting moves. As James followed along, he couldn't believe how lucky they were. Not only did they add another dancer, but they also were able to add some unique dance moves into their routine. Michelle's idea to incorporate everyone's moves was a great one, and it only proved to James how ready she was to be Dance Captain.

Eldon

Eldon wasn't sure what his status was with Emily. Today at dance she had let him carry her bag and get her a bottle of water. And just now at *Squeezed*, Emily had let Eldon buy her a juice. She even offered to sit with him while she drank it. She must have forgiven him for the duet debacle, Eldon thought; otherwise she wouldn't be spending so much time with me.

"I think if everyone keeps working hard, we have a really good shot at Regionals." Emily said.

Eldon barely heard her, he was too busy staring into her eyes-- her big, beautiful eyes.

"Eldon?" Emily questioned.

Quick, say something, Eldon thought to himself. "Yeah. Definitely." Eldon stammered. Agreeing with Emily was always the best course of action.

"So how are your brothers?" Eldon was surprised Emily was asking. She'd never done that before.

"They're good." Eldon told her. "We don't really talk much because we usually just stuff our mouths with food and play video games. Last week my mom came downstairs and we had all just fallen asleep in front of the TV. My brother still had chips in his mouth."

"Ew!" Emily laughed and covered her face.

She seemed to be genuinely having a good time with Eldon. It was almost as if she didn't hate him, even a little bit.

"You know what we should do?" Emily began, putting

her hand on Eldon's. "One weekend we should totally prank them. Wait until they fall asleep and put shaving cream in their hands and tickle their faces!" Emily joked.

But Eldon hadn't heard her speak. All he could think about was her hand resting softly on top of his. A few weeks ago she hadn't wanted to be within a mile of Eldon, and now here she was sitting with him in *Squeezed*, almost as if it were a second date.

Riley

R iley noticed Michelle had come back from *Squeezed* a little sadder than before she had left. She had happily offered to get them all juices, but now that she was back carrying several bottles, Riley could tell something had changed. "Hey, what's wrong?" Riley asked.

Riley may have only known Michelle for a month or two, but they had been spending so much time together she felt like she had known Michelle for much longer. And Riley knew Michelle wasn't fine.

"I saw Emily with Eldon in *Squeezed* and they looked pretty comfortable. I don't think we have to worry about her finding us in here." Michelle said.

Is that what this was about, Riley wondered. But was she upset about the Emily part? Or was she upset with the Eldon part? Or maybe it was the Emily with Eldon part?

"With West and all his tutting, this routine is going to be sick!" James said.

"I know!" Michelle said, brightening a little. "This thing," Michelle said, demonstrating a complicated sequence with her arms, "who could have thought of that except West?!"

"I know, right? Let's see Emily come up with something like that." James chimed in.

"What do you think Emily would do if she found out?"

Riley had been trying to avoid thinking about Emily at all, but now she gave it some thought. "She'd probably go to Kate." Riley said, finally.

"She'd probably rip my head off." James joked.

"She'd rip all of our heads off." Riley said, playing along. She felt more like herself around James and Michelle than she ever had around the E-Girls. She was glad that they were all in this together.

Then Riley heard their secret knock on the door. She, Michelle, West, and James had developed a secret knock that they had all promised to do before coming into Studio-B. In that way, they would know that whoever came in was a friend and not a foe.

"Come in!" Michelle yelled out happily.

West entered Studio-B like he was a secret agent on a spy mission.

"You guys," West began, "I sort of did something."

"Oh no," Riley thought, "what had West gotten up to now?"

"I told somebody about the dance." West finished.

"What? Who did you tell?" Riley demanded.

At that moment the door to Studio-B opened, and Riley couldn't believe who walked in through the door.

Daniel

D aniel stood in Studio-B waiting for someone to speak. West had told him about their plan and, although Daniel was interested, he wanted to make sure they all knew the consequences if it went awry.

"Riley, Emily is your sister. You know this is going to be war, right?" Daniel said, finally.

"Yeah. I do. But Emily does not deserve to be Dance Captain anymore. She is tearing us apart more than she is bringing us together." Riley said firmly.

Daniel had never been fond of Emily and how she treated people, and he was impressed with Riley for challenging her. He had always thought she would grow up to be like Emily, but she was turning out to be her own person, a good person.

"If I'm going to join, I have one condition." Daniel told them. "I get to keep my solo." Daniel knew that if he got a solo in this dance, it might lead to getting a solo in the real Regionals' dance.

"Of course!" Michelle, Riley, James, and West all said together. "We were kind of counting on it." Michelle told him.

Daniel smiled; it felt great to feel like he was wanted, not just tolerated. They all answered so quickly, he believed they meant it. And they did. "There is one other thing," Daniel said, "if we had one more girl we could do partnering and add lifts and stuff."

"Daniel's right. If we had one more person then we'd

have over half of A-Troupe on our side. That's a majority." Riley pointed out.

"Well, I know one thing for sure. It won't be Emily. The chances of her joining a dance to overthrow herself isn't very likely." West said seriously.

Everyone stared at West. What was West talking about? He might have magic feet, but his logic was anything but magical. Of course Emily would never join a dance to overthrow herself.

"That's true, West." Michelle said, kindly, holding back her smile.

"Thank-you, Michelle." West said politely back. He felt he was making a very good point.

Everyone laughed. If every practice was going to be this much fun, Daniel was glad he had chosen Michelle's team over Emily's.

"Oh no, you guys," Michelle said, looking at her phone, "we are missing rehearsal!"

"Do we really have to go back?" Daniel joked. But they all stood up and headed out of Studio-B. If their plan had any hopes of working, they all knew that Emily had to think everything was completely normal.

CHAPTER 21

Chloe

"Where is everybody?" Chris asked, coming into Studio-A from the office.

Chloe was surprised to see that Michelle, Riley, and James were late again. In fact, now that Chloe was looking around the studio, she noticed West and Daniel weren't there either. But a few seconds, later all five of them came running through the door.

"Thanks for making time for A-Troupe in your busy schedules." Emily almost hissed at the tardy dancers.

At least Emily wouldn't be mad at her for once, Chloe thought.

"Why don't we start from the ball-change-kick?" Emily told the dancers, counting them into the routine.

As everyone danced, Chloe took the opportunity to approach Chris about a new move she wanted to show him. Chloe thought it would demonstrate to everyone in A-Troupe that she was dedicated to dance.

Michelle

Meet me in Studio-B later.

Why?

I have something to show you. But it's a secret, please don't tell anyone.

I won't :)

Read 7:41PM

She had been working extra hard on a new move she thought would really improve the routine. Chloe wanted everyone to know that even if she was late for a practice, she was really working on dance every chance she had.

"I was thinking, instead of the ball-change-kick, we did a ball-change-jump. Instead of just a regular old kick." Chloe said, demonstrating as she spoke.

"That's a great idea." Chris said, "Can I see it again?"

"Sorry... I couldn't help overhearing." Chloe heard Emily say as she approached them. "As the Dance Captain, could I maybe see the new move you're proposing to add to my routine?" Emily asked, staring coldly at Chloe.

"I was just showing Chris." Chloe said, before demonstrating the ball-change-jump again. She hoped Emily liked it. It was a simple move, but it looked nicer than the usual ball-change-kick every studio would have in their routine.

"That's really pretty and looks great on you, but you should probably put it in one of your routines-- not one of my routines." Emily snarled at her.

Chloe was shocked. She hadn't meant to upset Emily; she just wanted to prove to everyone that she was a committed member of the team.

"Okay?" Emily asked Chloe, as if there was another

option.

"Okay." Chloe said, backing down.

"Okay!" Emily said, suddenly smiling again, "All right, everybody, let's take it from the ball-change-kick."

Chloe watched as Emily headed back to the front of the group and continued to lead rehearsal. She thought when Emily apologized it would be to start a whole new friendship, but now Chloe was starting to think things with Emily were never going to change.

Michelle

After Chloe had taken the brunt of Emily's outburst, Riley, Michelle, and James had all agreed that they should invite Chloe into their dance next. Michelle had texted Chloe after rehearsal and asked to meet her in Studio-B. And now Chloe was standing in Studio-B, watching them all dance.

As Daniel performed his solo, which they had added into the routine, Michelle looked over at Chloe. Everything seemed to be going well. Chloe was smiling and even clapping along to the music. Michelle hoped that they could convince her. They had taken a big risk by inviting her into their dance. She was an E-Girl after all. If she decided she didn't want to join them, she might tell Emily about everything and then their plan would be ruined.

"So, what do you think?" Daniel asked Chloe excitedly, once they had finished the routine.

"It's amazing. It's so good. What's it for? Is there a small group competition or something?" Chloe asked.

Michelle looked around at the other dancers. Someone had to tell Chloe the truth. It might as well be her. "It's for Regionals." Michelle said, coming clean to Chloe.

"I'm sorry, what?" Chloe asked. "Does Emily know about this?"

"Not exactly." Michelle said, shaking her head.

"And, we'd like to keep it that way." West said.

Michelle couldn't tell what Chloe was thinking, but she

didn't have to wait long to find out.

"Do you know how mad Emily would be if she found out you were choreographing a new dance behind her back?" Chloe challenged. "Do you? I'm sorry, but I'm not interested. And if you guys knew what was good for you, you wouldn't even be doing this." And with that, Chloe marched out of Studio-B.

"I knew that it was too soon to tell Chloe." Riley told them. "What if we just ruined everything?"

Michelle hated to admit it, but Riley was right. Their entire plan could have just been ruined.

"What are we going to do?" Riley asked Michelle.

"I'm sure she won't tell anyone." Daniel said to everyone.

"I'm not so sure." Riley said, disagreeing with Daniel. "This was clearly a mistake."

Everyone was quiet for a few moments. Michelle knew she had to fix this. She had been the one who had suggested telling Chloe in the first place. "I'm going to try talking to her." Michelle told the group. "And I'll just have to ask her not to tell anyone." As she headed out of Studio-B to find Chloe, Michelle hoped she sounded more positive than she actually felt.

CHAPTER 23

Stephanie

S tephanie was celebrating with Tiffany and Kate in Kate's office. Practice had ended hours ago, but she and Tiffany had stayed behind to wait for a call from a talent agent. And when it finally came, it was good news. The talent agency wanted to sign Stephanie and start sending her out on auditions!

Stephanie was hoping to become a triple threat: someone who can act, sing, and dance. She had always wanted to be more than just a dancer, and now she was well on her way to becoming the next big teen sensation. She had already picked out her stage name: Stephanie! With an exclamation point, and no last name.

But Stephanie wasn't a teen sensation yet. She was still just Stephanie. And plain old Stephanie knew something fishy was up the second she saw Chloe enter the studio. And she was even more suspicious when Michelle came in soon after and started talking to Chloe. Everyone else had gone home by now. Why were the two of them still there? Stephanie wished she had learned to read lips that summer her parents had sent her to sleepaway camp. That way she would be able to tell what Michelle and Chloe were saying to each other.

"We should probably get home, Miss Kate." Stephanie said, hoping to be able to get out of Kate's office before Michelle and Chloe left.

"Oh! You're right, look at the time!" Kate said. "Congratulations once again Stephanie! Both of you get home safe."

Stephanie jumped up, giving Tiffany a look to follow her. After all this time being E-Girls, they had come up with a few ways to communicate without saying a word.

"Hey, Chloe!" Stephanie said as she came out of the office.

"Hey." Chloe responded, looking startled. "What's up?"

Stephanie looked at Tiffany. Chloe was definitely hiding something.

"So what are you guys still doing here?" Stephanie asked, trying not to give herself away.

Before either girl could answer, the door to Studio-A creaked open, and Stephanie turned to see Riley and James step through it.

"Just rehearsing!" Chloe said quickly, trying to distract Stephanie from James and Riley's arrival.

But Stephanie wasn't falling for it. "And what are you guys still doing here?" Stephanie questioned James and Riley.

E-Girl Rule #23

An E-Girl is persistent: Ask questions, get answers.

"Rehearsing!" Riley was quick to answer.

"Yeah, they were all helping me." Chloe said.

"Without us?" Tiffany asked, saying exactly what Stephanie had been thinking.

"I couldn't find you guys. I'm sorry." Chloe apologized. "I'll definitely ask you guys next time."

Stephanie wasn't sure she should believe Chloe, and judging by the look on Tiffany's face, Tiffany felt the same way.

"Hey," Stephanie heard Kate call from inside the office, "it's getting late. Everybody go home!"

"Good idea!" Chloe said, grabbing her bag and hustling out of Studio-A. Michelle, Riley, and James all did the same thing, leaving Stephanie and Tiffany behind.

Stephanie looked at Tiffany, who rolled her eyes. "Do you believe them?" Stephanie asked her.

"Not for a second." Tiffany responded.

CHAPTER 24

Eldon

E ldon loved hanging out with James and West. They would spend hours in Studio-A trying to impress each other by throwing moves. Eldon remembered the day James landed the wall-flip for the first time and then spent the next four hours teaching Eldon and West how to do it, too.

"Check this out!" James said before throwing a double-leg; a jump where you whipped your body around while trying to keep both legs straight in the air.

"That was dope!" Eldon yelled to James when he landed.

"Okay, now show me that B-Twist!" James called back to Eldon. It was a move James could never seem to land.

"Okay, but I have to take off my socks first." Eldon said.

"Thank-you for the smell update." West said, and he and James burst into laughter.

Eldon didn't mind. James and West were his boys; their jokes were never mean-spirited.

"Okay. Let's see." West called out.

Eldon prepared himself and then sprung off the floor. Keeping his body flat and low, he flipped around quickly and landed on his feet.

"Woo!" West called out.

"Nice!" James agreed.

"It was a little low." Eldon said. He knew he was being critical of himself, but he knew it had to be perfect if he wanted Emily to be impressed.

"Don't worry, Emily will like it." James joked, knowing exactly what Eldon was thinking.

"How's it going with Emily, anyway?" West asked Eldon.

"I feel like we're getting more serious, but it's on the down low, you know?" Eldon was happy to talk about how well things were going with Emily.

"Really?" West said, holding back laughter.

"No you're not, man!" James said.

"We are though!" Eldon said, wondering why they didn't believe him.

"So you and Emily are legit? You guys are a couple?" West inquired.

"Well…" Eldon thought about it. "No, not right at this moment!"

"That's what I thought." West said, breaking into laughter.

"But we are getting close though!" Eldon continued. "And it's getting annoying that you guys don't believe me!"

"Eldon, you know we would love for you to finally get your chance with Emily. But it is not going to happen, bro." James replied, still laughing.

"Look, there's your girl now." West said, as Emily

entered Studio-A.

This was Eldon's chance to prove to his friends that things with Emily were better than they ever had been.

"Hey, Emily!" Eldon called with a smile. But Emily just looked at him as if he was someone she had never met before. On seeing that, West and James burst into laughter. "We are trying to keep it on the down low." Eldon said to his boys, trying to cover.

"Are you sure she even knows?" West said, laughing. "Because it seems to me like this is all in your head."

Eldon looked over at Emily. They had just had such a nice time at *Squeezed* and today she was ignoring him like it had never happened. Eldon had to do something to prove to everyone that this thing with Emily wasn't only in his head.

CHAPTER 25

Emily

E mily had left the studio early the night before because her mother had asked her to help with redecorating the living room. She was shocked to discover from Stephanie that Riley, James, and Chloe had stayed late to rehearse. After all, Riley had told her she was going to the movies. It was also very strange that Riley would lie about rehearsing. Emily knew she had to get to the bottom of things.

Emily found Riley in Studio-A hanging out with James and the boys. More often than not, wherever James was, Riley was nearby. Eldon called out to her, but she didn't have time to talk to him. She needed answers from Riley. "So… you weren't at dinner last night?" Emily began. She wanted to start slow. She couldn't let Riley know what she was doing. "Mom said you went to a movie?"

"Then you know where I was." Riley shot back, not wasting a second.

Emily had to admit that in the time she and Riley had spent apart, Riley had become a lot more independent.

"What movie did you see?" Emily asked.

Riley took a moment to answer. "That musical one."

"You hate musicals." Emily was on to something.

"What are you talking about, I love musicals." Riley said, smiling a fake smile.

Emily knew for a fact, Riley hated musicals. "Who did you go with?" Emily probed.

"I went with Michelle. She's really been opening my eyes to a lot of new things." Riley said.

"I didn't know you two were that close?!" Emily fished. If Riley was going to play games, then Emily could, too.

"Well, we are." Riley said flatly in response.

"What theatre did you go to again?"

"The Grand Theatre, theatre twelve. We had popcorn. Any more questions?" Riley asked, getting annoyed.

Emily noticed the other A-Troupe dancers had begun filing into the studio for rehearsal. "So you don't remember the name of the movie?" Emily asked.

"If you're so interested in the movie, you should probably go see it yourself. I didn't like it so much, but Michelle did." Riley said, smiling.

Emily was shocked at her sister's behaviour. A few months ago, Riley would have never even dreamed to speak to her that way. Now she was standing across the ballet bar from Emily, and Emily could barely recognize her. Riley had learned all of Emily's tricks and now she was using them against her. But Emily still had one more move.

"Rehearsal, now." Emily spat at Riley. "Rehearsal everyone, let's go boys." Emily said, turning to the rest of the dancers. If Riley thought she could beat Emily at her own game, she was horribly mistaken.

Riley

As rehearsal began, Riley found her way to Michelle. If Emily was questioning Riley about the movie, it wouldn't be long before Emily made her way to Michelle. Riley had to make sure their stories matched up. "By the way," Riley said, pretending to stretch near Michelle, "last night we saw the new musical at The Grand Theatre, theatre twelve. We had popcorn. You liked it, I didn't."

"Sweet." Michelle nodded at Riley, not wanting to say anything more, but totally getting it. If that's what she had to pretend they did the other day, so be it.

"Let's go!" Emily called out. "Everyone into position."

Riley took her place beside Tiffany in the back corner of the room. When the music began, she casually danced her way into the middle of the room. Riley was so bored of Emily's routine. It was so simple compared to Michelle's routine. Riley felt like she had gone back to Baby Ballet. All she wanted to do was get back to Studio-B, so she and the others could continue working on Michelle's routine and making it the best it could be.

"Michelle, watch those arms!" Emily called out.

Riley couldn't wait until they could show everyone their new routine, and then they wouldn't have to do Emily's anymore. As the dancers all moved into the group section of the dance, Riley noticed that West was doing the wrong choreography. Actually, he was doing the right choreography, but for the wrong dance. Instead of doing Emily's simple moves, West had launched himself into the group choreography for Michelle's dance. Please, please, please let Emily not notice.

"STOP!" Emily called out, pausing the music. "West!" Emily yelled.

But West wasn't stopping, he was going full out, dancing along to the music that had stopped playing more than ten seconds ago.

"West!" Emily yelled again, this time getting his attention. "That is not my choreography. What are you doing?" Emily demanded.

Riley stared at West, willing him to say something that made some sort of sense. Anything but the truth. Emily already thought something suspicious was going on with Riley and Michelle. If Emily connected West to them, everything would be over.

"What was that?" Emily asked again. She wasn't letting West off easy.

West looked around and then blurted, "Your choreography gets me so amped! It makes me want to…" West did a standing backflip. "It makes me just want to do that!"

Riley held her breath. The way Emily reacted would tell Riley everything.

"You want to do a backflip?" Emily asked, shaking her head. "No!"

Riley was relieved, Emily hadn't caught on. She just thought West was suggesting new moves for her choreography.

"If I wanted a backflip, I would have put a backflip in my dance." Emily hissed at West.

"You know what," West began, "you are so right. That is why you are Dance Captain."

Riley smiled to herself. West was so ridiculous that it actually worked in his favour.

"You don't have to remind me." Emily said. "First positions. We're doing this from the top." Emily marched back to the front of the room and started the music over.

As Riley started dancing again, she wondered how much longer they were going to be able to hide their plan from Emily. Either way, Riley was starting to think the sooner things changed, the better.

CHAPTER 21

Michelle

Michelle always asked her parents to pick her up an hour late, so she could finish her homework at *Squeezed*. If she finished it before she got home, she had more time to spend with her parents. She had been spending so much time at *The Next Step* lately that she had barely spent any time with her family. And she had been missing them a lot.

"Hi!"

Michelle looked up to see Emily sitting down across from her, a smile spread across her face. "Oh no," Michelle thought, "what was this about?"

"Hi?" Michelle replied, unsure of what Emily wanted.

"What are you doing?" Emily asked her.

Couldn't she tell? The textbook, blank paper; obviously Michelle was busy with her schoolwork.

"Math." Michelle responded without looking up. She wasn't going to let Emily sidetrack her. And a tiny part of Michelle felt that if she looked into Emily's eyes, Emily might just hypnotize her.

"The answer to that one is 'A'." Emily said, pulling Michelle's textbook towards her. "Just so you know."

"I know." Michelle told her. She didn't need Emily's help. Michelle had already had enough. She looked right at Emily. "What do you want, Emily?" Michelle asked. There was no need for them to pretend to be friendly when they so clearly were not friends.

"Oh, nothing." Emily said. "I just heard you went to a

movie with Riley yesterday."

"Yep." Michelle said, returning to her homework. So that's what this was about. Emily was trying to confirm Riley's story.

"So did you like it?" Emily asked.

Michelle knew Emily was on to them. Rather than answer all of Emily's questions, Michelle wanted to take control of the conversation.

"Why do you want to know?" Michelle asked.

"I'm just taking an interest in my sister and her little friends' lives." Emily said, trying to sound sweet, but coming off as rude.

"You've never taken an interest in my life. So why start now?" Michelle asked, closing her books. Michelle put her homework into her backpack and swung it over her shoulder. "I'll see you tomorrow." Michelle turned around and headed out of *Squeezed*, leaving Emily wondering what was going on. Michelle's hope was that if she acted as nonchalant as possible, it would throw Emily off the trail.

Emily

For the last hour, Emily had been pushing the team hard. "Five, six, seven, eight." Emily shouted out loud, as she watched A-Troupe perform the new part of the routine she had choreographed last night. As she watched everyone dance, she went over the facts as she knew them. She was sure something was going on, and Michelle's behaviour yesterday had proven it. If Michelle and Riley were trying to go behind Emily's back, then Emily wasn't going to give them the time to do it.

"Stop!" Emily commanded. "Chloe, you are a beat behind." Why was Chloe so behind if she had been staying late at the studio with Michelle and Riley to rehearse? "I am going to need more energy from all of you." Emily called out. "Five, six, seven--" But before she could get to eight, Eldon interrupted her.

"Why don't we take a fifteen minute break?" Eldon suggested.

"Sounds good!" West said, marching off the floor.

"I'm down." James agreed with him.

Emily watched the rest of the dancers fall out of formation. They didn't even wait for Emily to tell them it was okay to take a break. "Five! Five minutes. That's all!" Emily insisted.

"Hey, Emily." Eldon said, bringing Emily back from her stewing. "How's it going?" Eldon asked.

She wished she could tell him she thought Michelle and Riley were plotting against her, but even saying it in her head sounded too crazy to believe. "I was just thinking how great this shirt looks on you." Emily said. "Look we match." Emily held out her shirt to Eldon's.

"Shirt twins." he said, joking.

Emily laughed, she was getting used to his dopey jokes. She was even starting to like them. "Honestly, I am kind of worried. Everyone seems really tired. Do you know if anything is going on?" Emily questioned. If Eldon knew anything, he couldn't keep it from Emily.

"Nope." Eldon said with a smile.

It was time for Emily to pull out her secret weapon. "You know you can trust me, right?" Emily told Eldon, putting her hand on his shoulder.

"Yeah." Eldon said, looking down at her hand as if it were made of the most valuable substance in the world.

"You would tell me if there was anything going on, right?" Emily asked.

"Of course I would tell you." Eldon said, hugging Emily and holding on too tight.

Emily refused to close her arms around Eldon's back. He could hug her, but she was not hugging him back. She could hear the other E-Girls giggling across the floor. But then Emily saw Michelle's face. She had this oddly hurt look on her face. Emily closed her arms around Eldon, returning his hug. If hugging Eldon was going to upset Michelle, Emily could suffer through it. "Okay. All right." Emily said, pushing Eldon off. She wasn't willing to suffer that much. "I'm going to keep choreographing." Emily said, hoping Eldon would take the hint.

"Oh yeah, sorry. I'll go." Eldon said, heading towards the other boys.

"What was that about?" Chloe asked, running up with Stephanie and Tiffany. They had come to bother her about

Eldon, no doubt.

"Nothing. It was nothing." Emily insisted.

"It looked like you enjoyed that nothing." Chloe said, giggling along with Stephanie and Tiffany.

"Mind your own business, Chloe." Emily snapped. She knew the words were cruel when they came out of her mouth, but Chloe had pushed too far. Emily saw Chloe's face darken as she turned and walked away. Good, Emily thought, now they wouldn't bother her about Eldon.

CHAPTER 29

Chloe

C hloe marched into Studio-B knowing what she had to
do. She thought getting into A-Troupe would change
things with Emily, and that being an E-Girl would mean she
would be treated as if she belonged with the other girls.
But Emily was anything, but kind and welcoming. Chloe
knew nothing with Emily was ever going to change. So
she had to change things for herself. Chloe found Michelle
and the rest of the secret dance group practising their new
routine.

"What are you doing here?" Michelle asked.

The last time Chloe had seen this group together
she had told them to stop what they were doing. But now
Chloe felt differently. "Emily's reign as queen bee is over."
Chloe told the group.

"You want to join?" Michelle asked excitedly.

Chloe nodded. Riley ran towards Chloe and wrapped
her in a hug.

"I knew you'd come around." Daniel said.

Chloe was glad she had made this decision; she just wished she had made it sooner.

"So what changed?" James asked. Riley slapped his arm.

"It's okay. Nothing changed I guess. And nothing ever will change, as long as Emily is still Dance Captain." Chloe told them. "I thought I wanted to be an E-Girl." Chloe said, confiding in her new friends. "But now that I know what Emily is all about, I am so over it!"

"Are you being one-hundred percent serious?" West pressed, always finding the weirdest way to ask a question.

"One-hundred and ten percent." Chloe replied.

"Good choice." West held up his fist and Chloe bumped it with her own. Chloe had picked the right team.

"Let's start teaching you the choreo." Riley suggested.

The group spread out and Riley began showing Chloe the choreography they had so far. It was clear to Chloe that they had all had a say in the design of the dance. She could tell which moves were West's and which moves were Daniel's, but they all worked together to make a truly beautiful routine. Chloe couldn't wait to be a part of it. This idea of theirs might work after all, Chloe thought, glad she had come around when she did.

CHAPTER 30

Emily

Not only did Emily have to worry about Riley and Michelle, she also had to worry about Daniel. She had asked him to perform his solo so that she could see it, but he had hesitated. When he finally did dance, it was lazy. Daniel usually danced full out, but ever since he had gotten the Regionals' solo he had been slacking off. His dancing had gotten lazy and even now as he danced, Emily could tell he wasn't giving it his all. When he was done, Emily stepped towards him. "Daniel, just because you got the solo spot doesn't mean you can slack off, you know that right?" Emily questioned.

"Yeah." Daniel replied.

"I don't know what's going on, but you honestly need to fix it. You are replaceable as the soloist." Emily had to lay down the law. If Daniel couldn't get it together, she would have to find someone else to perform the Regionals' solo.

Emily was just about to say something else to Daniel when she heard music. Which was weird since she hadn't turned on the stereo. Emily looked up to see Eldon entering Studio-A with a boom box in one hand and several pieces of poster board in the other. Romantic music was playing, and Eldon had an odd look on his face. Emily wasn't sure what was going on, but it better have nothing to do with her.

"Emily." Eldon called out as he set the boom box on the floor. But before he could say anything, the CD began to skip, playing the same three words over and over again.

If this was Eldon's attempt at a romantic gesture, then he was getting every part of it wrong. Eldon kicked the boom box a few times until it began playing properly again. Once the song had resumed, Eldon flipped the poster board over, revealing a handwritten poem.

"There is no one else in the world," Eldon declared, reading the first poster board out loud, "that makes me feel the way you do!" Eldon called out, reading the second piece of poster board.

Emily looked around the room and saw James and West trying to suppress their laughter. This wasn't happening. Not right now. Not to her.

"Whenever you are gone, it makes me feel blue!" Eldon continued, letting each piece of poster board fall to the studio floor after he was done with it. "I will be there for you until the very end!" Eldon said, preparing for a big finish.

Emily's heart beat rapidly. She was flattered, but she was also unbelievably mad. Eldon was cute in private, but in public she still wanted nothing to do with him.

"Emily, will you be my girlfriend?" Eldon asked Emily, out loud, in front of all of A-Troupe.

Emily could hear everyone laughing now. How could

Eldon make her the laughing stock of the studio? Did he really think this was going to win her over? "What are you doing?" Emily shrieked, marching towards Eldon.

"Asking you out." Eldon replied, a little dumbfounded.

"Eldon. I will never be your girlfriend." Emily declared. "This is the most embarrassing moment of my life!"

Emily grabbed Eldon's final poster board and tore it in half. She knew she was being harsh, and she could see the hurt in Eldon's face, but Emily didn't have a choice. She had to let Eldon, and everyone else in A-Troupe, know that Emily and Eldon were not an item.

Eldon turned around and slunk out of the studio. Emily knew she had crushed him, but she couldn't care. Not right now. She had to save face. "Rehearsal positions, again!" Emily said, turning around to face her team. "Go!" she yelled, as the A-Troupe dancers took their places again. She wouldn't let this ruin rehearsal. She couldn't let this ruin rehearsal.

E-Girl Rule #16

An E-Girl will not be humiliated.

CHAPTER 31

Michelle

Michelle found Eldon sitting alone on the couch in Studio-B. She felt awful about the way Emily had treated him. What he had done for Emily was beyond anything Michelle could imagine. And Emily had acted like it was nothing. He looked so sad and hurt. "Hey, Eldon." Michelle said. Eldon looked up at her, his adorably sad face turned into a full-fledged frown.

"Oh, sorry, I didn't know anyone was going to be in here. I'll leave." Eldon said, getting up from the couch.

"No stay." Michelle said. "I came to talk to you." Eldon sat back down and crossed his arms. Michelle had never seen him this upset before. "Are you okay? I saw what happened earlier."

"Everyone saw what happened earlier." Eldon reminded her sadly. "I feel like the biggest dork."

"You're not a dork!" Michelle insisted.

"Well, according to Emily I am." Eldon said, crossing his

arms.

Michelle wished he could see what an amazing thing he had done. "Eldon, the things that you did for Emily were great. The poem and the music, it was so romantic." Michelle told him. She couldn't believe he thought any differently.

"Really?" Eldon asked, smiling.

"Really! If anyone did that for me, I would just melt!" Michelle said.

"I thought I was the only one who thought that was romantic." Eldon said, confiding in Michelle.

"I thought it was totally romantic." Michelle said quietly. For a moment she and Eldon shared a look.

"Hey, at least you spelled all the words right." Michelle joked, quickly changing the subject. Eldon barely laughed. It somehow reminded him of the humiliation.

This was as good a time as any to tell Eldon about their plan, Michelle thought. They may as well do it now, while Eldon remembered exactly how Emily had treated him. Michelle turned around and nodded to Riley, who had been watching through the window for Michelle's signal.

"Actually…" Michelle said, hearing the door to Studio-B open behind her. Riley, James, Chloe, Daniel, and West filed into Studio-B. "Eldon, we have something to show you." Michelle said, standing up to join the rest of her team.

CHAPTER 32

Emily

E mily listened to Stephanie and Tiffany make fun of Eldon as they sat at their table in *Squeezed*.

"When the boom box stopped working and he kicked it, and it just started playing a different song!" Tiffany said, gasping for air as she laughed.

"And it was, like, the least romantic song ever." Stephanie giggled along.

But Emily felt bad. She had been really mean to Eldon. Even though it was necessary, she wished things could have been different. Eldon had picked the wrong place and the wrong time to commit a PDA (Public Display of Affection), but maybe Emily could have handled things differently.

"What's your problem?" Stephanie asked after Emily hadn't said anything for a few minutes.

"Nothing. I'm just listening to you guys talk." Emily said, "It was just so funny. I'm still in shock."

"It was funny. It was the funniest thing I've seen in such a long time." Stephanie said, breaking into laughter again.

"Where's Chloe?" Emily asked, trying to change the subject. "Could you go look for her?" Emily asked Stephanie. Emily knew Stephanie hated to be sent on E-Girl errands, but Emily needed a break.

"Ugh. Fine." Stephanie said.

"Thanks." Emily said, smiling brightly at Stephanie. But she had so many other things on her mind.

E-Girl Rule #24

E-Girls need to stick together.

CHAPTER 33

Eldon

E ldon watched them perform their routine. It was so creative and different, he wasn't sure why they were showing him. They were using the same music Emily had chosen for Regionals, but it wasn't Emily's choreography at all. It was something new and different, and Eldon loved it.

"So, what did you think?" Michelle asked him as the dancers finished their performance. They all stood in front of him, breathing hard. They had danced all out, to try and impress Eldon.

"It was amazing!" Eldon replied. "What's it for?"

The other dancers all looked to Michelle. "It's for Regionals." Michelle told him. "Instead of Emily's."

Eldon was shocked. What did they mean, instead of Emily's? "Does she know about it?" Eldon asked. But he already knew the answer.

"No." West replied, seriously. Eldon had never seen West this serious before. In fact they were all serious. They

77

were going to replace Emily's routine with Michelle's.

"So?" Michelle asked, stepping towards him, "are you in?"

CHAPTER 34

Stephanie

Stephanie walked along the hallway. Chloe hadn't been in Studio-A, so Stephanie was going to pop her head into Studio-B before reporting back to Emily. Chloe had probably gone home. The last time Emily and Chloe had talked, it had ended with Chloe running out of the studio. Stephanie wouldn't hang around if she were Chloe. Or maybe Chloe was working on the Regionals' routine, because Stephanie could hear music coming from Studio-B. Good, Stephanie thought, Chloe needed the extra practice.

But when Stephanie peeked through the window into Studio-B, she didn't just see Chloe. Michelle, Riley, James, West, Daniel, and Eldon were there as well. And they were dancing to Emily's music. But they weren't dancing Emily's routine!

Stephanie pulled the door open quietly, making sure no one saw her. She watched for a few moments. This was definitely not Emily's routine. It had too many tricks and too

79

much hip-hop to be something Emily would choreograph. It looked like they had choreographed it all together. It showed off a little bit of everyone's talents.

Stephanie closed the door to Studio-B and ran back down the hall to *Squeezed*. She couldn't wait to tell Emily what she had seen.

"Did you find her?" Emily asked as Stephanie ran back into *Squeezed*.

E-Girl Rule #39

An E-Girl always reports gossip to all other E-Girls.

"Mhmm..." Stephanie said. "In Studio-B, dancing to your music, but not your choreography."

"With who?" Tiffany prodded.

"Daniel, West, Riley, James, and Michelle." Stephanie responded. She was happy to report back what she had seen.

"I knew she was planning something." Emily said finally.

Stephanie felt terrible for her best friend. They had all thought Michelle and Riley had been planning something, but now they had proof. And now they could do something about it.

CHAPTER 35

Emily

"Was Eldon there?" Emily asked. She had to know if he was against her, too.

"Who cares if Eldon was there?! Did you not hear what I just said?" Stephanie asked, incredulous that Emily would care about Eldon.

"Well, was he?" Emily demanded. She had to know if she had really hurt Eldon so badly that he had decided to join Michelle, whatever her plan may be.

"Yeah. He was." Stephanie informed her.

Emily never thought that it would be Eldon's betrayal that hurt her most. "Show me." Emily said. She had to see what was going on with her own eyes. They all immediately got up and headed off.

Emily marched down the hallway towards Studio-B, Stephanie and Tiffany doing their best to keep up with her. As Emily approached the door to Studio-B, she quietly put her hand on the doorknob, and slowly opened the door. She peeked her head through just enough to see Eldon.

He was standing across from Michelle and the other traitors.

"Emily just crushed your heart, how could you not want to join us?" James said.

"I couldn't hurt Emily like that. I'm not interested." Eldon said immediately in response.

Emily smiled. Maybe she hadn't completely lost Eldon. Not yet. Emily closed the door to Studio-B and gestured for Stephanie and Tiffany to follow her. "Let's go." she whispered to her friends. Emily had seen enough to know Eldon would never betray her. Now all she had to do was wait for Eldon to tell her what was going on, and Emily could go to Kate with the proof she needed. And Michelle would be gone from *The Next Step* forever.

CHAPTER 36

Stephanie

Stephanie stood at the ballet bar with Tiffany and watched as Emily talked to Eldon before rehearsal. They needed Eldon to spill the beans on Michelle so they could go to Kate with proof that Michelle really was a controlling diva. It didn't look like it was working very well, though. Eldon had just rolled his eyes and walked away from Emily, without saying a word about Michelle. Stephanie, gave a look to Tiffany, and the two of them headed over to Emily.

"Hey, girl, how are you love birds doing?" Tiffany joked.

"Love birds?! Please, I was pumping him for information." Emily told them.

"Yeah, right!" Stephanie didn't believe Emily for a second. Even though Emily had sworn she had absolutely no feelings for Eldon, Stephanie knew that wasn't true.

"We need to find a way to get Michelle out of the studio." Emily said, reminding Stephanie that they had bigger things to deal with than Eldon's crush on Emily.

"Yeah, but how?" Tiffany wondered, leaning back on the cubbies.

Stephanie noticed Michelle's bag lying open in her cubby. Stephanie reached her hand into the cubby.

"What are you doing?" Emily asked her.

"I have an idea." Stephanie said, pulling Michelle's phone out and beginning to type on it. Emily and Tiffany tried to look over Stephanie's shoulder to see what she was writing, but she wouldn't let them see. When Stephanie pressed the send button, Emily's phone began to vibrate.

"Looks like you got a text message. I wonder who it's from?" Stephanie said sarcastically.

Emily turned around and grabbed her phone from her cubby. As she read the message 'from Michelle', her eyes widened.

"That's so mean!" Emily said, showing it to Tiffany.

"You mean… so good!" Tiffany said, high-fiving Stephanie.

"I think I need to send you a few more texts." Stephanie said. And with that, she picked up Michelle's phone and started texting.

It was time for someone to do something about Michelle, and if no one else was going to do it, Stephanie would.

CHAPTER 37

Emily

E mily thought Stephanie's plan was brilliant. If they got away with it, it would be 'Bye, Bye' Michelle and 'Hello' old dance life. But if she was going to sell the lie, her performance had to be spot-on. Emily began sniffing as if she had been crying, before she walked sadly into Kate's office.

"What's going on Emily? Are you okay?" Kate asked.

Emily sat down across from Kate at her desk. "I don't even know if I should tell you this, Miss Kate." Emily began.

"Emily, what's up?" Kate said, worried.

"Remember when you told me to come to you about anything… like bullying going on?" Emily asked.

"Of course! Has someone been bullying you?" Kate asked, worriedly.

Emily prepared herself. "Michelle has been sending me really horrible text messages." she said, pulling out her phone and showing it to Kate.

Kate began reading through the text messages that Stephanie had sent to Emily. "Wow." Kate said, sounding disappointed. "Don't worry Emily, we're going to get to the bottom of this." She got up from her desk and looked out into the studio. "Michelle. In my office, now!" Kate called.

Emily fixed her hair, flicking it behind her shoulder, waiting for Kate to return with Michelle. Emily savoured these last moments of Michelle being at *The Next Step*. She was a formidable opponent, but she wasn't good enough to beat Emily.

When Michelle entered the office, Kate spoke first. "What do you have to say for yourself?" Kate asked Michelle.

"I'm lost?" Michelle said, honestly.

"Apparently you've been sending Emily not-so-nice text messages." Kate said, accusing Michelle.

Emily thought that was a bit of an understatement. "Horrible text messages." Emily clarified, but Michelle looked confused.

"I promise you I didn't do that. I would never do that!" Michelle insisted.

"It says it's from you, that's your phone number, right?" Kate asked, showing Michelle what was on Emily's phone.

"Listen, Michelle," Emily began, "here at *The Next Step Studio* we don't tolerate bullying. Right, Miss Kate?" Emily waited for Kate to back her up.

"You don't tolerate bullying? Really? Then why are you lying right now?" Michelle asked.

Emily had assumed Michelle would stick up for herself. But she didn't have a leg to stand on. "You sent those to me, and they really hurt my feelings." Emily said, putting on her best upset voice.

"She's lying to you! Because I don't even have my

phone." Michelle declared.

"What?" Emily shot, calling Michelle's bluff.

"It was stolen from my bag yesterday!" Michelle snapped back at Emily.

"Well, the only way we are going to solve this, is if we go look in your bag." Kate decided.

"Fine." Michelle said.

Emily led Kate and Michelle out into the cubby area.

"I can't believe I have to do this. My two best dancers, and I have to settle your disputes for you." Kate said, as she searched through Michelle's backpack. After rummaging around for awhile, Kate looked up. "It's not in here."

Emily grabbed the bag from Kate and began rummaging through it herself. It had to be in there. Where else could it have been, unless… and then Emily realized she had been played. Someone on Michelle's side had clearly figured out what Stephanie and Emily had done, and they had gotten rid of Michelle's phone. The other dancers had started to gather around the cubbies.

"Will somebody tell me what's really going on?" Kate asked.

If Kate really wanted the truth, Emily was happy to tell it. "Ever since Michelle has been here, things have been messed up." Emily said, turning to Michelle. "And now all of you are going behind my back to choreograph another Regionals' routine." Emily said, putting all of her cards on the table.

"Is this true?" Kate asked the group.

"Yes." Emily heard Riley say. So Riley was a part of it, too. Even though she suspected it, it was harder than Emily ever imagined to hear that Riley was a part of this betrayal.

Michelle

This was not how Michelle had wanted Kate to find out about their dance. She had wanted to do things in a respectful way, but Emily had made that impossible.

"And why are you choreographing a new routine?" Kate asked, still not understanding what was going on.

Michelle knew this was her chance to tell the truth. "Emily is a horrible Dance Captain." Michelle began, turning towards Emily. "You are bossy, rude, you yell at people, you don't include anyone else's ideas. And most important, you make everyone here feel like they would rather be anywhere else than dance."

"So what if I don't include other people's moves? They're not good moves." Emily sneered.

"A good Dance Captain doesn't tear her team apart." Michelle said, stepping towards Emily. She wasn't going to let Emily win this round. Because she knew this might be the final round.

"And you didn't tear things apart with this new routine of yours?" Emily snapped.

"I have had enough of this!" Kate declared. "The two of you have been fighting for long enough. It's time to put an end to it."

"Michelle, we'll watch your routine. At the end, everyone will vote on whether they want to keep Emily's original routine, and Emily as Dance Captain. Or change to Michelle's new one, making Michelle the new Dance Captain. Once that vote is done, this issue is done for good. Do you accept those terms?" Kate asked them.

"Yes." they both agreed.

"Good, then Michelle, let's see your routine."

Michelle headed into the middle of the studio with the rest of her dancers. They had worked so hard for this chance to overthrow Emily, but everyone knew it all came down to this one moment.

As the music began, James lifted Michelle in the middle of the floor and then placed her down beside Chloe and Riley. The three girls performed a ballet combo that Daniel had choreographed. As they cleared the floor, West sprung into a backflip, landing exactly beside where Miss Kate stood, giving her a quick smile. The dance moved into the salsa section, the same section West had begun dancing the other day in the middle of Emily's rehearsal. From there they began partner work, the three pairs all moving in unison. The dance continued with a hip-hop section West had choreographed, and then Daniel's solo.

Michelle was proud of how well this dance showcased everyone's talents. They had done exactly what they set out to do, and if Emily still won, then Michelle would know they tried their best.

CHAPTER 39

Emily

Emily still couldn't believe Michelle was actually trying to overthrow her as Dance Captain. But when she really thought about it, it wasn't as hurtful as knowing her own sister and all of the friends with whom she had grown up had gone behind her back. They had intentionally chosen the same song that Emily used for her routine to show off exactly how much better Michelle's dance was than Emily's. And it was better. So much better, Emily had to admit to herself.

As Michelle and the other dancers finished, Kate and Chris began clapping. "Nicely done." Kate said.

Emily got a sick feeling in her stomach. Almost everyone in A-Troupe had smiled to her face and then done the absolute best they could to take everything Emily had worked for, away from her. It stung Emily more than she wanted to admit.

She watched as Michelle's dancers all hugged and congratulated each other on a job well done. A few months ago they had all been her friends, and now they were nothing but enemies.

"So, who do you want to be your Dance Captain?" Kate asked all of A-Troupe. There was nothing left for Emily to do except stand there and wait.

The first person to vote was Stephanie. She moved across the floor and stood directly beside Emily. "You're my best friend. I've got your back, always." Stephanie whispered in her ear, hugging her. Emily smiled. She hoped some of the other A-Troupe dancers felt this way, but James and West quickly moved to stand behind Michelle. They were taking a side, and it wasn't Emily's.

Chloe followed behind them, stopping to say something to Emily. "For the longest time, I thought I wanted to be an E-Girl," Chloe said, "but now that I know what that really means, I am ready for something better."

E-Girl Rule #17

An E-Girl is loyal to the end.

Chloe's words hurt. Emily knew she had put Chloe through a great deal, but it had all been for Chloe's own good. After all, Emily was the one who convinced Chloe to try out for A-Troupe.

When Daniel chose Michelle, Emily began to realize the odds were no longer in her favour.

But when Tiffany started to move, Emily began to feel hopeful again. Tiffany was her friend and a fellow E-Girl. Of course she would choose Emily.

"Sorry." Emily heard Tiffany whisper, as she passed right by Emily and Stephanie, and settled behind Michelle.

"Seriously?" Stephanie shot at Tiffany. But Tiffany only shrugged. Yet Emily knew that it was the smart thing to do; Tiffany was only protecting her future.

The only two people left were Riley and Eldon. Emily knew Riley was going to choose Michelle, but that didn't make it hurt any less as she watched Riley cross the floor and stand defiantly behind Michelle.

Michelle had already won. Whoever Eldon chose

didn't really matter. But for some reason it mattered to Emily. His decision meant more to Emily than anyone else's.

Eldon stood there as if frozen. "Eldon," Kate prodded, "you have to vote."

Emily looked at Eldon, hoping he would meet her eyes, but he only looked at the ground. She had tried to apologize to him for everything she had done, but he wanted nothing to do with her. At any other time, Emily knew for sure that Eldon would be on her side, but right now she had no idea.

And then Eldon looked at her, right in her eyes. And before he even made a move, Emily knew she had lost. There were tears forming in her eyes by the time Eldon got to Michelle.

Was there anything she could have done to prevent this from happening? Could she have done things differently? It was too late to answer that. Her reign as Dance Captain was over. And it broke her heart.

CHAPTER 40

Michelle

"It looks like we have a new Dance Captain." Kate announced. "Congratulations, Michelle." Everyone began clapping and cheering.

"Thank-you." Michelle said to Kate and the other dancers. Michelle was proud of what she and the other dancers had accomplished. They had all worked together and done what was best for the team. For most of the team anyway.

"Emily, I hope now that this decision has been made you will be a team player, and I won't hear any more complaints out of you." Kate said pointedly to Emily. Emily quickly nodded and then let Stephanie guide her out of Studio-A.

Michelle thought for a moment about all the things that Emily had just lost and how quickly she had lost them. If it were Michelle, she would be on the floor crying, but Emily was still standing. In this moment Michelle was impressed with Emily's strength.

"I'm so happy! We're definitely going to win Regionals now!" Daniel said, giving Michelle a big hug.

"You are definitely the better Dance Captain." West joined in. "If there was a list of all the Dance Captains in the world, I bet you would be in the top five."

"Thanks, West." Michelle laughed. Michelle had never felt so happy and so sad at the same time. Their plan had worked. She was the new Dance Captain of *The Next Step* and they had a brand new Regionals' routine. A routine

that made everyone feel included and made everyone feel they were better dancers.

That's what Michelle should be feeling. But why did Michelle feel like, even though she had won the battle, there was still a war to come? This was definitely not the end of Emily.